W9-BGC-177

About this book

This book is for everyone who is learning their first words in German. By looking at the pictures, it will be easy to read and remember the words underneath.

When you look at the German words, you will see that in front of most of them is **der, die** or **das**, which means "the". When learning German, it is a good idea to learn the **der, die** or **das** which goes with each one. This is because all words, like table and clock, as well as man and woman are masculine or feminine, and some words, like bed, are neuter. **Der** means the word is masculine, **die** means it is feminine, and **das** means it is neuter. **Die** is also the word for "the" before plural words — that is, more than one, like tables or beds.

Most German words begin with a capital, or big, letter unlike most English words. There is also the letter ß in some words which is the same as "ss" written in English. On some vowels — a, o, and u — there are two dots, like this ä, ö, ü. This is called an umlaut and changes the way the vowel is said.

At the back of the book is a guide to help you say all the words in the pictures. But there are some sounds in German which are quite different from any sound in English. To say the German word correctly, you have to hear it said, listen very carefully and then try to say it that way yourself. But if you say a word as it is written in the guide, a German person will understand you, even if your German accent is not quite perfect.

THE FIRST HUNDRED WORDS IN GERMAN

Heather Amery

Illustrated by Stephen Cartwright

Translated by Anita Ganeri

There is a little yellow duck to find in every picture.

Das Wohnzimmer The living room

Vati
Daddy

Mutti
Mommy

der Junge
boy

das Mädchen
girl

2

das Baby
baby

der Hund
dog

die Katze
cat

Die Kleider Clothes

das Unterhemd
undershirt

die Unterhose
underwear

die Schuhe
shoes

die Socken
socks

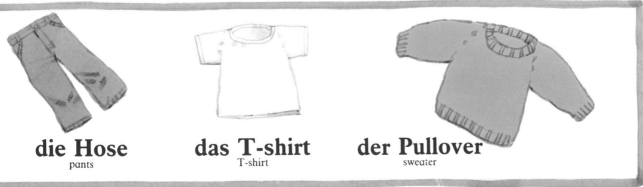

die Hose
pants

das T-shirt
T-shirt

der Pullover
sweater

In der Küche In the kitchen

das Brot
bread

die Milch
milk

die Eier
eggs

der Apfel
apple

die Orange
orange

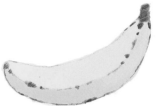
die Banane
banana

Der Abwasch Doing the dishes

der Tisch
table

der Stuhl
chair

der Teller
plate

das Messer
knife

die Gabel
fork

der Löffel
spoon

die Tasse
cup

Das Spielzeug Toys

das Pferd
horse

das Schaf
sheep

die Kuh
cow

das Huhn
hen

das Schwein
pig

der Zug
train

die Bausteine
blocks

Einen Besuch machen Going on a visit

Oma
Grandma

Opa
Grandpa

die Hausschuhe
slippers

12

das Kleid
dress

der Mantel
coat

die Mütze
hat

13

Im Park In the park

der Baum
tree

die Blume
flower

die Schaukeln
swings

der Ball
ball

die Rutschbahn
slide

der Vogel
bird

die Stiefel
boots

das Boot
boat

Auf der Straße

das Auto
car

das Fahrrad
bicycle

der Lastwagen
truck

16

der Bus
bus

das Flugzeug
airplane

das Haus
house

Die Party The party

das Eis
ice cream

der Kuchen
cake

der Ballon
balloon

18

die Uhr
clock

der Fisch
fish

die Kekse
cookies

die Bonbons
candy

Das Schwimmbad The swimming pool

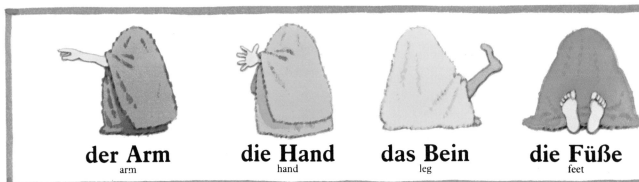

der Arm
arm

die Hand
hand

das Bein
leg

die Füße
feet

die Zehen
toes

der Kopf
head

der Hintern
bottom

21

Der Umkleideraum The changing room

der Mund
mouth

die Augen
eyes

die Ohren
ears

die Nase
nose

die Haare
hair

der Kamm
comb

die Bürste
brush

Das Geschäft The store

rot
red

blau
blue

grün
green

gelb
yellow

rosa
pink

weiß
white

schwarz
black

Das Badezimmer The bathroom

das Bad
bathtub

das Handtuch
towel

die Toilette
toilet

die Seife
soap

der Bauch
tummy

die Ente
duck

Das Schlafzimmer The bedroom

das Bett
bed

das Fenster
window

die Tür
door

die Lampe
light

das Buch
book

die Puppe
doll

der Teddy
teddy

Match the words to the pictures

der Apfel

das Auto

der Ball

die Banane

das Buch

das Ei

das Eis

die Ente

das Fenster

der Fisch

die Gabel

der Hund

die Katze

der Kuchen

die Kuh

die Lampe

das Messer

die Milch

die Mütze

die Orange

der Pullover

die Puppe

das Schwein

die Socken

die Stiefel

der Teddy

der Tisch

die Uhr

das Unterhemd

der Zug

Die Zählung Counting

1 eins one   **2 zwei** two   **3 drei** three   **4 vier** four   **5 fünf** five

First published in 1988. © Usborne Publishing Ltd. Printed in Spain.

Words in the pictures

In this alphabetical list of the words in the pictures, the German word comes first, next is the guide to saying the word, and then there is the English translation. Although some German words look like English ones, they are not said in the same way. And some letters have different sounds. In German, w sounds like English v, v sounds like f, z like ts, and j like y in yellow. There are also some sounds in German which are quite different from any sound in English.

The guide is to help you say the words correctly. They may look strange or funny but just read them as if they are English words, remembering these special rules:

ah is said like *a* in *farther*
a is said like *a* in *add*
ow is like *ow* in *cow*
e(w) is different from any sound in English. To make it, say *ee* with your lips rounded.
ee is like *ee* in *week*
ay is like *ay* in *day*
y is like *y* in *try*, except when it comes before a vowel. Then it sounds like *y* in *yellow*.
g is like *g* in *garden*
kh is like *ch* in the word *loch* or the *h* in *huge*.
r is rolled at the back of your mouth
er is like *er* in *butter*

German	Guide	English
der Abwasch	*derr abvash*	doing the dishes
der Apfel	*derr apfel*	apple
der Arm	*derr arm*	arm
die Augen	*dee owgen*	eyes
das Auto	*dass owto*	car
das Baby	*dass baby*	baby
das Bad	*dass bahd*	bathtub
das Badezimmer	*dass bahder-tsimmer*	bathroom
der Ball	*derr bal*	ball
der Ballon	*derr ballon*	balloon
die Banane	*dee bananer*	banana
der Bauch	*derr bowkh*	tummy
der Baum	*derr bowm*	tree
die Bausteine	*dee bow-shtine*	blocks
das Bein	*dass bine*	leg
das Bett	*dass bet*	bed
blau	*blaow*	blue
die Blume	*dee bloomer*	flower
die Bonbons	*dee bonbons*	candy
das Boot	*dass boat*	boat
das Brot	*dass broat*	bread
das Buch	*dass bookh*	book
die Bürste	*dee bewrster*	brush
der Bus	*derr booss*	bus
drei	*dry*	three
das Ei	*dass eye*	egg
die Eier	*dee eyer*	eggs
eins	*ynss*	one
das Eis	*dass ice*	ice cream
die Ente	*dee enter*	duck
das Fahrrad	*dass fahr-raht*	bicycle
das Fenster	*dass fenster*	window
der Fisch	*derr fish*	fish
das Flugzeug	*dass floog-tsoyk*	airplane
fünf	*fewnf*	five
die Füße	*dee foosser*	feet
die Gabel	*dee gahbel*	fork
gelb	*gelp*	yellow
das Geschäft	*dass gay-sheft*	store
grün	*grewn*	green
die Haare	*dee hahrer*	hair
die Hand	*dee hant*	hand
das Handtuch	*dass hant-tookh*	towel
das Haus	*dass house*	house
die Hausschuhe	*dee house-shooer*	slippers
der Hintern	*derr hintern*	bottom
die Hose	*dee hoze*	pants

German	Pronunciation	English	German	Pronunciation	English
das Huhn	*dass hoon*	hen	das Schaf	*dass shahf*	sheep
der Hund	*derr hoont*	dog	die Schaukeln	*dee showkeln*	swings
			das Schlafzimmer	*dass schlarf-tsimmer*	bedroom
der Junge	*derr yoonger*	boy	die Schuhe	*dee shooer*	shoes
der Kamm	*derr kamm*	comb	schwarz	*shvarts*	black
die Katze	*dee katser*	cat	das Schwein	*dass shvine*	pig
die Kekse	*dee kekser*	biscuits	das Schwimmbad	*dass schvim-bahd*	swimming pool
das Kleid	*dass klyt*	dress			
die Kleider	*dee klyder*	clothes	die Seife	*dee zyfer*	soap
der Kopf	*derr kopf*	head	die Socken	*dee zocken*	socks
die Küche	*dee kewkher*	kitchen	das Spielzeug	*dass shpeel-tsoyk*	toys
der Kuchen	*derr kookhen*	cake	die Stiefel	*dee shteefel*	boots
die Kuh	*dee koo*	cow	die Straße	*dee shtrasser*	street
			der Stuhl	*derr shtool*	chair
die Lampe	*dee lamper*	light			
der Lastwagen	*derr last-vahgen*	truck	die Tasse	*dee tasser*	cup
der Löffel	*derr lurfel*	spoon	der Teddy	*derr teddy*	teddy
			der Teller	*derr teller*	plate
das Mädchen	*dass mayt-khen*	girl	der Tisch	*derr tish*	table
der Mantel	*derr mantel*	coat	die Toilette	*dee twaletter*	toilet
das Messer	*dass messer*	knife	das T-shirt	*dass tee-shirt*	T-shirt
die Milch	*dee milkh*	milk	die Tür	*dee tewr*	door
der Mund	*derr moont*	mouth			
Mutti	*mootee*	Mummy	die Uhr	*dee oor*	clock
die Mütze	*dee mewtze(r)*	hat	der Umkleideraum	*der oom-klider-rowm*	changing room
			das Unterhemd	*dass oonter-hemt*	vest
die Nase	*dee nahzer*	nose	die Unterhose	*dee oonter-hoser*	pants
die Ohren	*dee oren*	ears			
Oma	*ohmar*	Granny	Vati	*fartee*	Daddy
Opa	*ohpar*	Grandpa	vier	*feer*	four
die Orange	*dee oranjer*	orange	der Vogel	*derr fogel*	bird
der Park	*derr park*	park	weiß	*vyss*	white
die Party	*dee party*	party	die Wohnzimmer	*dee vone-tsimmer*	living room
das Pferd	*dass pfert*	horse			
der Pullover	*derr pool-ofer*	jumper			
die Puppe	*dee pooper*	doll	die Zählung	*dee tsahl-oong*	counting
			die Zehen	*dee tsayen*	toes
rosa	*roza*	pink	der Zug	*derr tsook*	train
rot	*roat*	red	zwei	*tsvy*	two
die Rutschbahn	*dee rootsch-bahn*	slide			

First published in 1988. Usborne Publishing Ltd. Usborne House, 83–85 Saffron Hill, London ECIN 8RT. © 1991, 1988, Usborne Publishing Ltd.